Nora
the Arctic Fox
Fairy

Special thanks to Narinder Dhami

ISBN 978-0-545-70856-2

12 11 10 9 8 7 6 5 4 3 2 1   15 16 17 18 19/0

Printed in the U.S.A.   40

First Scholastic printing, January 2015

Nora the Arctic Fox Fairy

by Daisy Meadows

SCHOLASTIC INC.

The Fairyland Palace

Meadow

Stream

Beehive

Arctic Tundra

Eucalyptus Forest

Tropical Waterfall

Wild Woods
Nature
Reserve

Jack Frost's
Ice Castle

To Jack Frost's Zoo

Watering Hole

Pagoda

Desert Oasis

I love animals—yes, I do,
I want my very own private zoo!
I'll capture all the animals one by one,
With fairy magic to help me get it done!

A koala, a tiger, an Arctic fox,
I'll keep them in cages with giant locks.
Every kind of animal will be there,
A panda, a meerkat, a honey bear.
The animals will be my property,
I'll be master of my own menagerie!

Contents

Moonlight Magic

"Isn't it a beautiful evening?" Rachel
Walker remarked to her best friend,
Kirsty Tate. They stared up at the night
sky dotted with tiny, glittering stars.
The evening air was warm and still, and
above the trees the moon shone with a
pale, silvery light.

"It's a perfect way to end our week at
Wild Woods," Kirsty agreed. The girls

had volunteered to spend part of their summer vacation at the nature reserve near Kirsty's home, learning how to be junior rangers. Now it was their last day, and all the volunteers were waiting outside the wildlife center for Becky, the head of Wild Woods, to join them for a special evening.

"It's really nice of Becky to take us on a moonlit walk," Rachel said. "I hope we see lots of different animals."

"Becky said it was a special treat because we'd all worked so hard," Kirsty reminded her. "Even though we also have our badges as proof!"

Both girls gazed proudly at the pockets of their backpacks, which were covered with badges. Every time they'd completed their tasks successfully, Becky had given them a badge, and the girls had six so far.

There was a murmur of excitement as Becky hurried out of the wildlife center, carrying a bag of equipment.

"We have a wonderful evening for our walk," Becky said. "But to make the most of it, you'll all need one of *these*!" She took a flashlight out of the bag and turned it on. Rachel and Kirsty were surprised to see the flashlight glow red.

"These flashlights have special red filters that allow you to see in the dark," Becky went on, handing the flashlights out. "But they won't disturb wildlife like a bright yellow beam would. So keep your eyes peeled for animals that only come out at night!"

"And we should keep our eyes peeled for fairies, too!" Kirsty whispered to Rachel excitedly.

While they were working at the nature reserve, the girls had also been helping the seven Baby Animal Rescue Fairies. The fairies had been busy protecting wildlife from Jack Frost and his goblins. When Rachel and Kirsty arrived at

Wild Woods, they'd been delighted
to meet their old friend from Fairyland,
Bertram a frog footman. Bertram had
taken them to visit the Fairyland Nature
Reserve, but Jack Frost and his goblins
turned up to ruin everyone's fun. Jack
Frost had announced that he wanted
animals for his very own zoo! With one
bolt of icy magic from his wand, he'd
stolen the Baby Animal Rescue Fairies'
magic, animal-shaped key chains. Then
Jack Frost had given the special charms
to his goblins and sent them spinning
away to the human world. He had
ordered the goblins to find animals for
his zoo.

Rachel and Kirsty had offered to help
the Baby Animal Rescue Fairies get
their key chains back, so the fairies

worked their magic and gave the girls the power to talk to animals.

"It's been so much fun talking to all the animals we've met," Rachel said as everyone followed Becky into the woods. "And the magic has helped us rescue six baby animals from Jack Frost and his goblins, too."

"Now we only have Nora the Arctic Fox Fairy's key chain to find," Kirsty pointed out. "Then all wildlife will be safe from Jack Frost, and the animals won't end up in his private zoo!"

"Let's stay a little behind the others," Rachel suggested. "Just in case we *do* meet a fairy!"

Becky led the junior rangers down a winding path through the trees, with

Kirsty and Rachel at the rear. Suddenly, they heard a hooting noise.

"Hoo! Hoo!"

"An owl!" Becky declared, her eyes gleaming with excitement. "Keep still, everyone."

Seconds later a brown and white owl swooped past them, its amber eyes glinting in the moonlight. Everyone gasped with delight.

The owl landed in a tree near the girls, and gazed down at them.

"Lovely evening," the owl hooted softly.

"Yes, it is," Kirsty murmured, hoping the others wouldn't hear.

After walking for a short distance, Becky came to another stop. "Here are some tracks in the dirt," Becky said, pointing at the ground. "Can anyone guess what animal made these footprints?"

The junior rangers gathered around her. Rachel and Kirsty were about to join them when they heard a noise in the bushes close by.

"It was *I* who made those tracks!" whispered a deep voice.

Rachel pointed her flashlight into the undergrowth. The girls saw a badger sniffing around in the leaves, his eyes bright in the moonlight.

"Oh, hello!" Kirsty said.

"Good evening," the badger replied, scurrying busily away.

"We'd better go," Rachel said, noticing that Becky and the others had moved on.

Rachel turned off her flashlight. As she did, Kirsty spotted the glimmer of something deep in the undergrowth. It was glittering in the moonlight. Kirsty wondered if it was another animal. But, if so, what on earth could it be?

"Rachel, there's something sparkly among the leaves!" Kirsty whispered.

This time both girls turned their flashlights on. And there, in the red glow, they saw Nora the Arctic Fox Fairy perched on a branch right in front of them!

"Hello, girls!" Nora called. She waved up at them and grinned.

Paw Prints in the Snow

"Have you been expecting me, girls?" Nora asked, twirling up into the air. She wore a blue dress printed with red hearts, and a snug vest made of white faux fur. The ends of her long blond hair were dip-dyed gorgeous shades of pink and purple.

"We *have* been
looking for you,
Nora," Kirsty
replied.

"We only
have one key
chain left to find
now," Nora said,
landing on Rachel's
shoulder. "*Mine!* Girls,
I need your help. A little
fox cub named Dazzle has gone missing. I
don't know if Jack Frost has anything to
do with her disappearance, but we *must*
find Dazzle and bring her safely home."

"Of course!" Kirsty replied. "We're
ready!" The girls turned off their
flashlights and with one flick of Nora's
wand, fairy sparkles floated gently down

around them. Then Rachel and Kirsty
were lifted off their feet and swept far
away from Wild Woods.

Just a heartbeat later, the girls found
themselves in an icy, frozen land. The
snow-covered ground glittered beneath
the moonlit sky, and a harsh wind
was blowing, whipping up flurries of
snowflakes in the distance.

"Where are we?" Kirsty asked. She was glad that Nora's magic had provided both girls with hooded parkas, wool-lined boots, and cozy hats, scarves, and mittens.

"I thought foxes lived in forests or fields," Rachel added, puzzled. She couldn't see a single tree or plant anywhere on the frozen landscape.

"Girls, this is the Arctic tundra," Nora explained. "Arctic foxes live near the North Pole, and the ground is frozen here for most of the year. Not much can grow."

Kirsty could see tracks in the thick snow around her feet. "These are paw prints," she said, looking more closely. "And they're fairly small, too. I wonder what animal made them."

"Let's follow the trail," Nora suggested.

The girls walked across the crisp, deep snow, Nora flying alongside. After a few moments they arrived at a mound of snow with a small hole dug in the side.

"This is a fox's den," Nora told them.

"I think Dazzle and her family live here. Let's go inside."

Nora shook her wand and a few fairy sparkles, shining brightly against the white snow, tumbled gently onto Rachel and Kirsty. Immediately, the girls began to shrink, stopping only when they were the exact same size as Nora herself.

The three of them flew into the foxhole. As they moved along the network of

tunnels, going deeper underground,
Kirsty was surprised by how warm and
sheltered it felt beneath the blanket of
thick snow.

At last, they reached the den. Rachel
exclaimed in delight as she spotted four
fox cubs cuddled together, their long,
fluffy tails curled neatly around them.
The cubs had thick fur, as white as the
snow, and adorable little faces with small
black noses and bright black eyes.

"Hello, cubs," Nora said. "Has Dazzle come home yet?"

The cubs looked worried.

"No, she hasn't," the biggest cub squeaked anxiously.

"And we can't tell our mom because she's out hunting," added one of the others.

"We'll find Dazzle and bring her home," Nora told the fox cubs.

"Thank you!" they barked in chorus.

Nora and the girls said good-bye to the fox cubs and then set off through the maze of tunnels again. When they reached the surface, Kirsty zoomed out of the hole first, only to be hit by a swirling mass of snow that knocked the breath out of her.

"Oh!" Kirsty gasped, realizing it had begun snowing heavily while they

were inside the
hole. She tried to
flutter upward,
but the snow was
falling so thickly,
it was impossible
to fly. The huge
snowflakes
knocked Kirsty out
of the air, forcing her
to land on the ground. Rachel
and Nora fought their way through the
blizzard and joined her.

"What are we going to do?" Rachel
panted despairingly, shaking the snow
from her hood. "How on earth are we
going to find Dazzle if we can barely get
off the ground?"

Sled Ride

Kirsty, Rachel, and Nora stared at one another in dismay. Then, to her surprise, Kirsty heard the sound of jingling bells, followed by the noise of dogs yapping.

"Someone's coming!" Kirsty said breathlessly.

Rachel peered through the whirling snowflakes. She could just make out a wooden sled pulled by dogs skimming

across the snow. A young Inuit boy
dressed in warm clothes was holding the
dogs' reins, urging them on.

"Maybe he
can help us,"
Rachel suggested eagerly.

Nora nodded. "Quickly, girls, let me
turn you back to your human size before
he disappears!" she said.

The girls immediately ducked behind
a snowdrift so that Nora could work

her magic. Then they waded out again,
hoping the boy hadn't gone very far. To
Rachel's relief, she saw that the sled had
stopped nearby.

"Good luck, girls," Nora told them.
"I'd better hide!"

Rachel tucked the little fairy safely
inside her hood. Then she and Kirsty
hurried through the falling snow
toward the
boy. He was
speaking to
his dogs,
patting their
heads, one
by one.

"Hello!" Kirsty
called, brushing the
snowflakes from her nose.

The boy turned and gazed at them in surprise. "Hello," he replied. "I wasn't expecting to meet anyone! Who are you?"

"I'm Rachel, and this is Kirsty," Rachel explained.

"I'm Miko," the boy said, his dark eyes warm and friendly. "I'm going to visit my grandmother, but I think something's wrong with one of my dogs."

Kirsty glanced at the dogs. They had thick brown and white fur and curling tails, and they looked fit and strong, but Kirsty could hear one of them whimpering softly.

"Oh, my paw really hurts!"

Rachel heard it, too, and she and Kirsty exchanged a knowing glance.

"Maybe I could check the dogs for you, Miko," Kirsty suggested.

"Thank you," Miko said gratefully.

While Kirsty went to find the injured dog, Rachel stayed with Miko. "This place is amazing," Rachel said as more snow settled around them, glittering like white diamonds in the silver moonlight.

"There's so much snow and ice! Does it ever melt?"

"Yes, in summer the snow disappears," Miko explained. "The summer season is very short here, but the sun shines all the time, even at midnight!"

"That's amazing!" Rachel gasped.

"Something even more amazing happens here in winter," Miko told her. "If you're lucky, you can see the Northern Lights!"

"The Northern Lights?" Rachel repeated.

"It's a big, colorful display of lights in the night sky," Miko said. "My dad explained to me exactly how nature makes the Northern Lights happen, but I just like to think of it as something magical and beautiful."

By now Kirsty had found
the whimpering dog.
She knelt down
next to him.

"What's the
matter?" Kirsty
whispered, concerned.

"I have something stuck in my paw,"
the dog panted, holding up one of his
front legs. "Please help me!"

Gently, Kirsty checked the dog's paw
and right away she spotted a sharp sliver
of ice stuck in his soft pad. Grasping the
ice with her mittened hand, she eased it
out carefully.

"Thank you!" the dog barked.

"Your dog's fine now," Kirsty called
to Miko. "He had some ice stuck in his
paw, but I took it out."

"Poor Shika!" Miko hurried over to pat the dog. "Thank you, Kirsty. I'm sure Shika would say thank you, too, if he could."

Kirsty laughed. "Yes, I'm sure he would!" she agreed.

"Now, is there anything I can do to help *you*?" Miko asked. "I see you don't have a sled. Can I take you somewhere?"

"We're searching for a missing fox cub," Kirsty explained. "Would you help us look for her?"

"Of course!" Miko agreed eagerly.

Then Rachel heard Nora whisper urgently to her from inside her hood.

"Rachel, look—in the distance!"

The snow had stopped falling now and Rachel could see across the frozen plain.

There, silhouetted against the stark white landscape, she could see another sled zooming along. This sled was nothing like Miko's simple wooden one, though— it was blue, and much fancier. Rachel could see that the sled was decorated with glittering icicles twisted into wintry shapes. The driver was wearing a coat with a hood pulled over his face as if to disguise himself, but Rachel could see he was tall and thin with a long nose and a frozen beard.

"Look, Kirsty, it's Jack Frost!" Rachel gasped. "I bet he kidnapped Dazzle!"

"Let's go after him!" Miko cried.

Rachel and Kirsty jumped onto the sled behind Miko. He gathered up the reins and called out to the dogs, who immediately took off, pulling the sled along with them. Kirsty gasped as the freezing wind whirled around them, turning her cheeks red. She was utterly

amazed at the speed they were traveling
as they glided smoothly across the snow,
the dogs running as fast as they could.

"We're catching up!" Rachel said as
they got closer to Jack Frost's sled.

As Miko got closer to Jack Frost, Kirsty
leaned forward to look into the other
sled. She caught a glimpse of a ball of
white fur on the seat next to Jack Frost.

"It's Dazzle!" Kirsty gasped.

Dazzle in Distress

"STOP!" Rachel yelled at the top of her lungs. "Let that little fox cub go!" Jack Frost turned and shot her a freezing glare, but he didn't stop.

"No way!" Jack Frost roared. He was so loud he scared Miko's dogs, and they started barking. "My useless goblins were lousy at collecting animals, so I decided to get one for myself! And an Arctic fox is the perfect creature for the zoo at my Ice Castle!"

"What's he saying?" Miko asked. "I can't hear because of the dogs."

"He wants the fox cub for his zoo," Kirsty explained.

"His zoo?" Miko exclaimed, shocked. "That's terrible!"

"How can we get Dazzle back,

Kirsty?" Rachel wondered as Jack Frost yelled at his dogs to go even faster.

Kirsty thought hard as Miko's dogs, unsettled by Jack Frost, continued to bark noisily. Suddenly, the dogs themselves gave her an idea.

"Rachel, I'm sure Jack Frost's dogs would stop if we told them their master had kidnapped a little fox cub!" Kirsty whispered hopefully. "But we'd have to do it without Miko seeing that we can talk to animals."

"Great idea," Rachel agreed. "I'm sure we could find a way to distract Miko." She suddenly remembered her conversation with Miko earlier and smiled. "I think I know how!"

Quickly, Rachel took off her hood and Nora peeked out.

"Miko told me the Northern Lights are magical and amazing," Rachel went on. "I'm sure they would distract him while we try to rescue Dazzle!"

"Let's see what I can do," Nora whispered, pointing her wand at the black night sky.

The girls watched a shower of dazzling sparks burst from the wand like an exploding firework. Immediately, great ribbons of green light tinted with pink and violet formed across the sky, swirling and dancing in the darkness like giant flames.

"Look, Miko!" Rachel shouted, pointing at the sky.

"It's the Northern Lights!" Miko
gasped excitedly, slowing the sled down
to get a better look.

"Let's go, girls," Nora said. One wave of her wand transformed Rachel and Kirsty into fairies once more. Then they zoomed off toward Jack Frost's sled, while Miko stopped and gazed in awe at the spectacular lights above them.

Jack Frost had also slowed down a little to enjoy the magical display. He was so entranced, he didn't notice the fairies fly past him. "This light show must have been put on in my honor!" Rachel heard him murmuring boastfully.

Nora and the girls flew until they were right above the dogs pulling the sled.

"Please stop!" Kirsty begged them. "Your master has kidnapped a baby animal!"

"Kidnapped?" all the dogs barked together in amazement, and they came

to a dead stop. They stopped so suddenly that Jack Frost was almost thrown out of the sled.

"Come on, move!" Jack Frost shouted, shaking the reins. "MOVE!" But the dogs stayed where they were. Grumbling loudly, Jack Frost climbed out of the sled, leaving Dazzle huddled miserably on the seat.

"Let the fox cub go!" one of the dogs yelped, and the others barked loudly in agreement.

"You dogs are as useless as my silly goblins!" Jack Frost clapped his hands over his icy ears.

As Jack Frost continued to rant at the dogs, Nora flew silently over to the sled to check on Dazzle. Kirsty and Rachel were following her when Kirsty glanced down and spotted something furry sticking out of one of the pockets of Jack Frost's coat.

"It's Nora's magic key chain!" Kirsty whispered to Rachel.

"Let's grab it!" Rachel suggested.

The Seventh Key Chain

The girls fluttered down behind Jack
Frost so he couldn't see them.

"How dare you disobey me!" Jack
Frost shrieked at the dogs. He was
having a tantrum now and stamping his
feet in the snow. "I *order* you to move!"

"Not until you let the fox cub go," the
lead dog barked.

Kirsty and Rachel hovered beside Jack Frost's pocket. They were so close to Nora's furry, fox-shaped key chain, they could see the faint magical glow that surrounded it.

"NOW!" Kirsty whispered. She and Rachel darted forward and together they lifted the key chain gently out of Jack Frost's pocket. Carrying it between them, they flew straight over to Nora, who was talking softly to a weary Dazzle. Nora stared at the charm as if she couldn't believe her eyes, and her face lit up with pure joy.

"Aren't you clever, girls!" she declared.
"Where did you find it?"

"In Jack Frost's pocket!" Rachel replied
as she and Kirsty handed her the key
chain. The very second Nora touched it,
the key chain magically shrank to its
fairy-size.

"I want my mom,"
Dazzle squeaked.
"I don't like that
frosty man!"

"We'll take
you home
to your mom,
Dazzle," Nora
told her. She showed
the fox cub her charm.
Dazzle cheered up immediately when
she saw its magical glow. Eagerly, she

jumped out of the sled. Unfortunately, at that moment, Jack Frost happened to glance around. His face darkened when he spotted Nora, Rachel, and Kirsty.

"I'm fed up with fairies!" Jack Frost roared. "Always following me around, sticking your nose into my business!" He charged toward them, trying to swat Nora and the girls away. "And keep your hands off that fox cub—she's going to be the prize exhibit in my special zoo!"

Skillfully, Nora, Rachel, and Kirsty avoided Jack Frost's flailing arms and flew back toward Miko's sled. Dazzle also dodged Jack Frost and scampered after them, her eyes fixed on the key chain Nora was holding. Miko was still gazing rapturously up at the colorful display in the sky and didn't even notice when Dazzle jumped into his sled. Then Nora waved her wand, and her magic quickly restored the girls to their normal size.

"I'm tired of you fairies always messing everything up!" Jack Frost howled, stomping around in frustration and kicking snow everywhere.

"You shouldn't have tried to steal animals for your horrible old zoo, then!" said Rachel.

"You can't just collect animals like marbles," Kirsty reminded him. "Animals need to be treated with love and care."

"Oh, how boring!" Jack Frost sneered. "Why do you fairies *always* have to spoil *all* my fun?" Still complaining, he

vanished in a shower of icy magic.
Smiling happily, Rachel and Kirsty
climbed into Miko's sled.

"Thank you for your help, girls," Nora
said gratefully, landing on Rachel's
shoulder. She pointed her wand up at the
sky again and, as the
lights began to fade,
she snuggled down
into Rachel's scarf,
out of sight.

"That was the
most amazing
Northern Lights
display I've ever seen!"
Miko turned to look at the girls, his
eyes wide with excitement. "It was so
magical, I even thought I saw some
fairies flitting around in the night sky!"

"Oh, you probably just saw some snowflakes," Rachel said quickly.

"Or maybe it was us!" Kirsty whispered in her ear.

Then Miko noticed Dazzle on the seat next to him. "And you found the missing fox cub!" he exclaimed, stroking Dazzle's thick fur. "Should we take her home?"

"Yes, please!" Dazzle squeaked.

"Yes, please, Miko," Rachel said, winking at Kirsty.

Swiftly, Miko released Jack Frost's dogs and hitched them to his own sled. Then they sped off across the snowy plain, back toward the den. As they got closer, Dazzle began to get very excited.

"Hooray!" she barked. "I'm going home!"

Miko stopped the sled outside the den

and Dazzle, Rachel, and Kirsty jumped
out together.

"I need to go straight to my
grandmother's," Miko said. "I'm very
late. Good-bye to you all!"

Rachel and Kirsty thanked Miko
and waved as the boy shot away across
the snow. Then Dazzle raced toward the
hole, but before she reached it, her brothers
and sisters came tumbling out. They
were followed by their mother, home
from hunting.

"Dazzle's home!" the cubs barked in chorus, rushing to nuzzle noses with their sister.

"Thank you *so* much," the mother fox said as Dazzle nestled against her. "I've been very worried about her."

"She's safe now," Nora told them. "And I'll see you again very soon!" She turned to the girls and raised her wand. "Now, I think we should go back to the Fairyland Nature Reserve and tell everyone we've found my key chain at last!"

As Dazzle and her family called good-bye, a flash of sparkles from Nora's wand circled Rachel and Kirsty and carried them away from the snowy land. In the twinkling of an eye, the girls and Nora arrived at the Fairyland Nature Reserve where a crowd had

gathered to meet them. All the other Baby
Animal Rescue Fairies were there, as
well as King Oberon and Queen Titania.
Rachel and Kirsty were also delighted to
see Bertram the frog footman, Fluffy the
squirrel, and Queenie the bee.

"Look!" cried Kitty the Tiger Fairy. "Nora has her key chain back, which means our magic is complete once more!"

"Now we can protect wildlife everywhere again," Mae the Panda Fairy said happily.

There were cheers and everyone applauded loudly. Then Queen Titania stepped forward. "Girls, we thank you for coming to our rescue," she said with a sweet smile. "You have proved yourselves to be true friends over and over again."

"We're glad we could help," Rachel told her. "And we *did* have lots of fun talking to the animals!"

"Yes, we really loved it," Kirsty added. "But we know the magic can't last now that all the Baby Animal Rescue Fairies have their key chains back again."

"Well, maybe the magic can last for a *little* while longer," the queen replied. "Long enough for you two girls to join us for a celebration party with the animals here at the Fairyland Nature Reserve, maybe?"

There were more cheers as the girls glanced at each other in delight.

"We'd love to!" said Rachel.

"And thank you very much, Your Majesty!" Kirsty added.

Farewell to Wild Woods

The party at the Fairyland Nature
Reserve was so enchanting, Rachel and
Kirsty really didn't want to leave. The
Party Fairies had done all the organizing.
They'd decorated the nature reserve with
lanterns and candles, and they'd hung
sparkly lights in the trees. The Music
Fairies played beautiful music, and there
was a huge table with delicious food,

including seven spectacular frosted cakes shaped like the Baby Animal Rescue Fairies' key chains. The girls had a wonderful time dancing with the fairies and chatting with the different animals who all came to thank them for helping to keep them safe.

But at last it was time for the girls to return to Wild Woods, and everyone gathered to see them off.

"Once again, girls, all our thanks,"
King Oberon said warmly. "Enjoy the
rest of your last evening at Wild
Woods!"

"We will!" Rachel said.

"Good-bye, everyone," Kirsty called
as Queen Titania pointed her wand
at them.

"Good-bye! Good-bye!" With the
shouts of their fairy friends ringing in
their ears, the girls were whisked away
by the queen's magic. Almost instantly
they found themselves back in the woods.
Ahead of them they could see Becky
leading the others to a clearing on the
side of a hill. Rachel and Kirsty rushed
after them.

"What an amazing adventure!" Kirsty
said breathlessly.

"It was fantastic!" Rachel agreed, her eyes shining.

When they reached the middle of the clearing, there was a fabulous view of the black night sky with the big full moon and silver stars overhead.

"And now I want to present you all with one final badge as a reward for completing the week's work," Becky announced, and she held up a big, star-shaped gold badge with JUNIOR RANGER written on it.

Rachel and Kirsty were thrilled as they lined up to receive their badges with the other volunteers.

"Now you're all officially junior rangers!" Becky laughed as, bursting with pride, the girls pinned their badges to the middle of their backpacks. "I think we should celebrate." Becky began to hand out brownies and cups of hot chocolate.

"We've had *two* celebrations today." Rachel sighed happily, sipping her hot chocolate. "How great is that?"

But Kirsty was staring toward the edge of the clearing. "Look, Rachel," she whispered softly. "Some of our friends are here!"

Rachel looked and saw the owl they'd met that evening, sitting in a tree. He was hooting softly, but now, of course, the girls couldn't understand what he was saying. The badger they'd seen earlier was sniffing around the bottom of the tree, and as the girls watched, the shy little fawn they'd made friends with a few days ago appeared. Then rabbits and squirrels started popping out of the undergrowth, staring at the girls with bright eyes.

"I think they've come to say good-bye!" Rachel guessed.

"And there's something else, too . . ." Kirsty pointed out seven tiny, twinkling lights flitting among the trees.

"Could they be the Baby Animal Rescue Fairies?" Rachel breathed excitedly. "Oh, Kirsty, I can't *wait* for our next magical adventure with our fairy friends!"

SPECIAL EDITION

Don't miss any of Rachel and Kirsty's
other fairy adventures!
Check out this magical sneak peek of

Carly
the School Fairy!

Competition Countdown

Rachel Walker strolled over to the grand doors of Tippington Town Hall and peered outside. There were buses pulling up and lots of people milling around, but no sign of the very special person she was looking for, her best friend, Kirsty Tate!

Rachel's school was taking part in an exciting competition. Four schools from different parts of the country were competing in two different events; a spelling bee was going to be held today at Tippington Town Hall and a science fair was to take place at the Science Museum tomorrow. At the end of the week, there would be a dance at Rachel's school!

Rachel was part of the Tippington School spelling bee team, but the *most* exciting thing was that Kirsty's school was also taking part in the competition. Kirsty was part of the science team and this meant that she was coming to Tippington!

"Rachel! Over here!" called Kirsty. Rachel turned around and there was Kirsty! She was standing with three

other children and a friendly-looking
teacher.

"There you are! I was wondering when
you'd get here!" said Rachel, running
over to Kirsty and giving her a big hug.

"We came in through the side
entrance," said Kirsty with a smile. "This
is my teacher, Mrs. Richards, and this is
my science team!"

Just then, an official-looking man in a
fancy suit appeared on the stairs leading
up to the auditorium. "Attention please,
everyone! I am your host for today's
competition. Will the four teams taking
part in the competition please make their
way to the backstage area? Members
of the audience should take their seats in
the auditorium."

The four spelling bee teams started to make their way to the backstage area.

"I'll join you in a minute!" Rachel called to her team. "I'm just going to walk Kirsty to her seat."

The girls split off from the main group of students and teachers in the hall, and made their way toward a side entrance. As they strolled along, something in one of the trophy cases caught Kirsty's eye. "Rachel, what *is* that?" she asked, stepping closer.

"It's just the light shining on the Tippington in Bloom cup, isn't it?" replied Rachel, still walking toward the auditorium.

"I think it's something even more special than that!" whispered Kirsty

happily, tugging on Rachel's arm.
Rachel stopped suddenly. There, sitting
on the edge of a shiny trophy surrounded
by a magical glow, was a beautiful
little fairy!

RAINBOW magic™

Which Magical Fairies Have You Met?

- ❏ The Rainbow Fairies
- ❏ The Weather Fairies
- ❏ The Jewel Fairies
- ❏ The Pet Fairies
- ❏ The Dance Fairies
- ❏ The Music Fairies
- ❏ The Sports Fairies
- ❏ The Party Fairies
- ❏ The Ocean Fairies
- ❏ The Night Fairies
- ❏ The Magical Animal Fairies
- ❏ The Princess Fairies
- ❏ The Superstar Fairies
- ❏ The Fashion Fairies
- ❏ The Sugar & Spice Fairies
- ❏ The Earth Fairies
- ❏ The Magical Crafts Fairies

■ SCHOLASTIC

Find all of your favorite fairy friends at
scholastic.com/rainbowmagic

HIT entertainment

RMFAIRY